To Pauline

100 Powerful *Prayers*

In the Presence of God

Let each prayer take you into the presence of God

Carol Clarke

100 POWERFUL PRAYERS
IN THE PRESENCE OF GOD
Copyright © 2020 by Carol Clarke

All rights reserved. This book or any portion thereof may not be reproduced or used in any manner whatsoever without the express written permission of the publisher except for the use of brief quotations in a book review.

CONTENTS

Acknowledgements 7
To The Reader 8
A prayer about BREAK-THROUGH 10
A prayer about HEALING 11
A prayer about DELIVERANCE 12
A prayer about FAMILIES 13
A prayer about REJECTION 14
A prayer about MOTHERS 15
A prayer about FATHERS 16
A prayer about PARENTS 17
A prayer about RESTORATION 18
A prayer about STRENGTH 19
A prayer about FINANCIAL BLESSING 20
A prayer about ENCOURAGEMENT 21
A prayer about GOD'S WILL 22
A prayer about PURPOSE 23
A prayer about PROMOTION 24
A prayer about INFERTILITY (BARRENNESS) 25
A prayer about VISION 26
A prayer about OVERCOMING GRIEF 27
A prayer about SELF-CONTROL 28
A prayer about UNDERSTANDING 29
A prayer about PATIENCE 30
A prayer about COMPASSION 31
A prayer about CAREER ACHIEVEMENT 32
A prayer about OVERCOMING PAST FAILURES 33

A prayer about BETRAYAL 34
A prayer about JOB PROSPERITY 35
A prayer for STRENGTH FOR THOSE IN DEBT 36
A prayer of STRENGTH FOR THOSE WHO ARE SICK 37
A prayer about FEELING UNLOVED 38
A prayer about THE HOMELESS 39
A prayer about THE LOST 40
A prayer about MARRIAGE 41
A prayer about DEALING WITH OVEREATING 42
A prayer about PEACE 43
A prayer about ENDURANCE 44
A prayer about LOVE 45
A prayer about KNIFE CRIME ADDICTS 46
A prayer about GOVERNMENT 47
A prayer about FINANCIAL MIRACLE 48
A prayer about HEALING FROM CANCER 49
A prayer for GOOD WEATHER 50
A prayer about COURT VICTORY 51
A prayer WHEN IN FEAR 52
A prayer about EMOTIONAL STABILITY 53
A prayer about SURGERY 54
A prayer about BAD DREAMS 55
A prayer about KNIFE CRIME VICTIMS 56
A prayer about PRESSURES AT WORK 57
A prayer about IDENTITY 58
A prayer about DEALING WITH CONFRONTATION 59
A prayer about CHEMOTHERAPY PATIENTS 60
A prayer about FORGIVING YOURSELF 61

A prayer about RACIAL HEALING 62
A prayer about SUICIDAL THOUGHTS 63
A prayer about DECISION MAKING 64
A prayer about MENTAL ILLNESS 65
A prayer about FINDING A LOVE RELATIONSHIP 66
A prayer about NEWBORN BABIES 67
A prayer about A SON AND DAUGHTER 68
A prayer about GRIEF AND COMFORT 69
A prayer about RENEWAL OF YOUTH 70
A prayer about LONGEVITY 71
A prayer about COMMUNITY INVOLVEMENT 72
A prayer about SPEAKING IN TONGUES 73
A prayer about FAITH 74
A prayer about CHURCH LEADERSHIP 75
A prayer about THE BODY OF CHRIST 76
A prayer about BOLDNESS TO PROCLAIM THE GOSPEL 77
A prayer about PASTORS 78
A prayer about ACTIVATING YOUR SPIRITUAL GIFT 79
A prayer about WISDOM 80
A prayer for CHILDREN TO SAY 81
A prayer about DISCERNMENT 82
A prayer about CHRISTIAN VALUES 83
A prayer about THE HOLY SPIRIT 84
A prayer about COMMITTING PLANS TO GOD 85
A prayer about MONEY AND STEWARDSHIP 86
A prayer about THANKING GOD IN ADVANCE 87
A prayer about SALVATION 88
A prayer about BLESSINGS 89

A prayer about DYING WITHOUT JESUS 90
A prayer about FORGIVENESS OF SINS 91
A prayer about HABITUAL SIN 92
A prayer about SPIRITUAL AUTHORITY 93
A prayer about CHURCH MINISTRIES 94
A prayer about THE GIFT OF PROPHECY 95
A prayer about THE ANOINTING OF GOD 96
A prayer about REVELATION 97
A prayer for THE START OF A MEETING 98
A prayer for THE END OF THE MEETING 99
A prayer about TEACHERS 100
A prayer about WOMEN IN BUSINESS 101
A prayer about BUSINESS OPPORTUNITIES 102
A prayer about SUCCESS 103
A prayer about A HUSBAND BLESSING HIS WIFE 104
A prayer about A WIFE BLESSING HER HUSBAND 105
A prayer about A FATHER'S BLESSING OVER HIS SON 106
A prayer about A FATHER'S BLESSING OVER HIS
    DAUGHTER 107
A prayer about A MOTHER'S BLESSING OVER HER
    SON 108
A prayer about A MOTHER'S BLESSING OVER HER
    DAUGHTER 109

ACKNOWLEDGEMENTS

First, I would like to give thanks to God The Father, The Son and The Holy Spirit, because without Your revelation and direction this book would not have been possible.

Different people have been key contributors to this book and I extend my gratitude and thanks to them.

To my husband Rob Clarke, thank You for believing in me and standing with me in this ministry. Thank You for being my spiritual watchman and partner in ministry. Thank you to my three children Chanel, Benjamin and Dominique, who God has passed on the mandate, enabling her to write some of these powerful prayers.

To my parents, Clarinston and Pernella King, who has supported me both financially and prayerfully. To my siblings, Maxine Mukuna, Zena Senior, Sharmaine King; brother-in-law, Shaun Senior, aunties, uncles, nieces, nephews and other relatives, thank you. I also extend thanks to my Church family - The Church of God of Prophecy, Cattell Road, Small Heath, Birmingham. Thank you for your encouragement and prayerful support.

This book is dedicated back to God, who has revealed Himself to me through prayer. These prayers are written with the intent to empower others in prayer and that God is revealed personally.

TO THE READER

How many times have we heard that prayer is talking to God? Prayer in fact goes deeper than just talking to God. Pray is the language of heaven. Prayer is not only talking to God but also listening to Him; it is hearing what the Spirit is saying to your spirit. God is interested in every area of our lives and wants that every junction we face, every road we cross, every dual carriage we journey, He is in the driving seat. Therefore, communicating with God through prayer will enable us to build a deeper and meaningful relationship with Him, giving him access in every area of our lives.

Perhaps, you have experienced situations in your life for years and need God's guidance and direction in your personal prayer life. So to every reader, this book is for you. God is not looking for us to repeat the same prayers over and over again; otherwise we become like sounding brass or a clanging cymbal. By including 100 unique prayers covering different topics, this prayer book will increase your prayer life and revitalise your relationship with God. Praying each topic based on your own personal circumstances and situations will help you to draw closer to God.

To pray these prayers, you can pray them in order of which they are written, or based on your personal situations; alternatively, you can use the table of contents to pray an urgent prayer topic. As you seek to develop your prayer life, as you pray these prayers, apply the *Lectio Divina* model to each prayer:

- *Pray each prayer slowly*
- *Meditate on what is being prayed*
- *Slowly read and reflect on the Word of God*
- *This whole process becomes a prayer*
- *As you pray, let the prayer become the gift of enjoying the presence of God*

You can use these prayers to help pray for others. Also, the shorter prayers in this prayer book can be used perhaps before work or early morning when time is limited.

As you join this journey of deepening your prayer life, our goal is that as you pray these prayers each and every day, your desire for communicating with your Heavenly Father will be ignited, in turn drawing closer to him.

As you pray these prayers, let the will of God be made manifest in your life; let His divine glory be revealed to you. As you call to Him in your time of prayer, believe that He will answer. As you pray, He has promised to show you great and mighty things, which you did not know (Jeremiah 33:3).

It is always an honour to be given access into the presence of God. Through a heart of prayer, you have been given the opportunity to enter into the secret place of the Most High God; that only comes to those who are willing and desire communication with God.

Let's take this journey of prayer together and let's begin.

A PRAYER ABOUT BREAK-THROUGH

Heavenly Father, I thank you for break-through in my life and I am assured that I walk in victory and not defeat. I bless you because I am fruitful and not fruitless; happy and not sad. Therefore, I pray that You will continue to help me live a life of forgiveness from a life of sin as I reach new levels of spirituality. So, I thank you for Your Word that declares that no weapon formed against me shall prosper. I pray that you will help me to rise above failures and negative criticisms and through the work of the Holy Spirit, I will experience Your presence in every situation, in Jesus Name, Amen.

"No weapon formed against you shall prosper, and every tongue which rises against you in judgment You shall condemn. This is the heritage of the servants of the Lord, and their righteousness is from Me," Says the Lord. **Isaiah 54:17**

Carol Clarke Ministries

A PRAYER ABOUT HEALING

Father, we thank You for Your Word that reminds us that 'by Your stripes we are healed'. Therefore, we pray this prayer of healing, believing that You are able to do exceedingly abundantly more than we could ever ask or think. So, we thank You for your healing powers that flow within every organ of our body which is the temple of the Holy Spirit. We believe and trust in You, knowing that there is no sickness or condition greater than your power to heal in Jesus Name, Amen.

But He was wounded for our transgressions, He was bruised for our iniquities; The chastisement for our peace was upon Him, And by His stripes we are healed. **Isaiah 53:5**

Now to Him who is able to do exceedingly abundantly above all that we ask or think, according to the power that works in us. **Ephesians 3:20**

A PRAYER ABOUT DELIVERANCE

Dear Jesus, we thank You because You are never too tired of hearing our cry. We have every confidence that we can cast our cares upon You because You care for us. Therefore in our daily challenges and overwhelming situations help us to remember Your Word, which reminds us that "You are our hiding place; You will protect us from trouble and surround us with songs of deliverance" So Father, deliver us from fear, doubt, oppression, depression, unforgiveness, malice, anger, anxiety and worry and clothe us with love, joy, peace, gentleness, kindness, faith, meekness and temperance in Jesus Name.

Casting all your care upon Him, for He cares for you. **1 Peter 5:7**

You are my hiding place; You shall preserve me from trouble; You shall surround me with songs of deliverance. **Psalm 32:7**

But the fruit of the Spirit is love, joy, peace, longsuffering, kindness, goodness, faithfulness, gentleness, self-control. Against such there is no law. **Galatians 5:22-23**

Carol Clarke Ministries

A PRAYER ABOUT FAMILIES

Lord we pray for your divine covering and blessings upon our families. We pray that you will bind us together with chords that cannot be broken. So, Father, help us to love and appreciate one another. Unify us with your love; unite us with Your peace and divine blessing. Will You shine your light upon us and give us Your supernatural strength in challenging and difficult situations? We pray that You will forgive us of all sins that displease You, Amen.

Bearing with one another, and forgiving one another, if anyone has a complaint against another; even as Christ forgave you, so you also must do. 14 But above all these things put on love, which is the bond of perfection. **Colossians 3:13-14**

A PRAYER ABOUT REJECTION

Dear Father, throughout my life, I have had to deal rejection and to be honest this has negatively impacted my life in so many ways. Lord, I find it hard to accept true friendships or even relationships because I tell myself they too will reject me. But Lord I stand on Your word that even though I am rejected by humans, I am chosen by God and precious in your sight. So Lord, I come to You, because You are the living Stone; thank You heavenly Father, Amen.

Coming to Him as to a living stone, rejected indeed by men, but chosen by God and precious. **1 Peter 2:4**

Carol Clarke Ministries

A PRAYER ABOUT MOTHERS

Dear God, I dedicate this prayer to all mothers. May the Lord bless every mother (birth and spiritual mothers), with the gift of the Holy Spirit. Lord, I pray that You will cover them with peace and love that surpasses all understanding. Bless them for the love and support they so freely give to others. May every mother never doubt or lack self-worth, but know that nothing will separate them from your love; thank You Lord, Amen.

And the peace of God, which surpasses all understanding, will guard your hearts and minds through Christ Jesus. **Philippians 4:7**

A PRAYER ABOUT FATHERS

Dear Father, we thank You for fathers and the role they play in the life of their child/children. God, we recognise that fatherhood is not an easy task, but we thank You for the example You left in Your Word that states as a father has compassion on his children, so the Lord has compassion on those who fear him. May the Lord bless ever father and that they may be strengthened in their inner being. May they prosper and be in good health. Lord may you keep every father safe; let Your face shine upon them and be gracious to them. May You lift up Your countenance upon fathers and give them peace. Amen.

As a father has compassion on his children, so the LORD has compassion on those who fear him. **Psalm 103:13**

Carol Clarke Ministries

A PRAYER ABOUT PARENTS

Heavenly Father, I thank You for the gift of parenting (natural and spiritual parents). Lord, may You Lord bless every parent in all that they do and for the support and love they show to their children. Reign down Your blessings upon them, and I pray that You bless them with long lives and good health both physically and spiritually. May You always protect them and keep them in Your tender care, granting them courage and confidence and provision. Lord, let every parent bear much fruit as they continue to be good stewards over their children in which you have entrusted in their care. Help every parent to prove faithful in their God given responsibilities, thank You Lord, Amen.

Moreover, it is required in stewards that one be found faithful.
1 Corinthians 4:2

A PRAYER ABOUT RESTORATION

Father we thank you for being the Father of love, comfort, joy, peace and restoration. We thank You for restoring to us the years the swarming locust has eaten. We therefore proclaim that we will not be ruled by forces of darkness or spiritual wickedness in high places because the blood of Jesus has set us free. We proclaim that the God of love will go before us throughout this year and season in Jesus Name we pray Amen.

So I will restore to you the years that the swarming locust has eaten, The crawling locust, The consuming locust, And the chewing locust, My great army which I sent among you. **Joel 2:25**

Therefore, if the Son makes you free, you shall be free indeed. **John 8:36**

A PRAYER ABOUT STRENGTH

Heavenly Father, I thank You that you are the joy of my strength. For this reason, I will push through, even though my inner thoughts tell me to quit. I bless You because I am strong in the Lord when in the valley of the shadow of death and in weakness, then I am made strong. Help me Lord to condition myself to draw on the God given strength to overcome all adversities and redefine who I am in Christ Jesus, Amen.

"...Do not sorrow, for the joy of the Lord is your strength." **Nehemiah 8:10**

Yea, though I walk through the valley of the shadow of death, I will fear no evil; For You are with me; Your rod and Your staff, they comfort me. **Psalm 23:4**

Therefore, I take pleasure in infirmities, in reproaches, in needs, in persecutions, in distresses, for Christ's sake. For when I am weak, then I am strong. **2 Corinthians 12:10**

A PRAYER ABOUT FINANCIAL BLESSING

Dear Father, thank you for all that you have given me. Despite my financial position, I know that I am blessed and ask that You will help me to make wise and prudent financial decisions according to Your plan for my life. Lord I pray that I will not spend out of contentment but condition me to be content in every financial situation. Remove from me every worry and anxious thoughts about money and replace them with trust and faith in You. I bring the whole tithe into the storehouse, and I am confident that You will open the windows of heaven and pour a blessing until it overflows in Jesus Name, Amen.

Bring all the tithes into the storehouse, That there may be food in My house, and try Me now in this," Says the Lord of hosts, "If I will not open for you the windows of heaven And pour out for you such blessing That there will not be room enough to receive it. **Malachi 3:10**

Carol Clarke Ministries

A PRAYER ABOUT ENCOURAGEMENT

Heavenly Father, I thank you because it is in You that I find reassurance and help in a world full of uncertainty. I am encouraged by Your Word that declares that You give strength to the weary and You increase power of the weak. So, I will not be discouraged; I will not doubt or fear because those who hope in the Lord will renew their strength. Therefore, I declare that I shall soar on wings like eagles; I shall run and not grow weary, I will walk and not be faint, in Jesus Name, Amen.

Have you not known? Have you not heard? The everlasting God, the Lord, The Creator of the ends of the earth, neither faints nor is weary. His understanding is unsearchable. He gives power to the weak, and to those who have no might He increases strength. Even the youths shall faint and be weary, and the young men shall utterly fall, But those who wait on the Lord Shall renew their strength; They shall mount up with wings like eagles, They shall run and not be weary, They shall walk and not faint. **Isaiah 40:28-31**

A PRAYER ABOUT GOD'S WILL

Dear Father, I thank You that my life is in Your hand and I am directed and guided by You. So, let Your will be done in my life and let Your kingdom come here on earth as it is in heaven. I, therefore, trust in You Lord with all of my heart; I will not depend on my own understanding, but I will seek Your will and purpose in all that I do because I know that You will show me which path to take in Jesus Name; thank You Lord, Amen.

Your kingdom come. Your will be done On earth as it is in heaven. **Matthew 6:10**

Trust in the Lord with all your heart, and lean not on your own understanding; In all your ways acknowledge Him, and He shall [a]direct your paths. **Proverbs 3:5-6**

A PRAYER ABOUT PURPOSE

Dear Lord, I thank You for giving me a purpose-filled life. From this day, I choose to walk in purpose for that which I have been called. I shall be fruitful and multiply and will fill the earth and subdue it because I have been given dominion over it. Therefore, I shall rise and stand upon my feet, for You have appeared to me for this purpose, to appoint me as a servant and witness to the things of God. This is the prayer of my heart, thank Your Father, Amen.

But rise and stand on your feet; for I have appeared to you for this purpose, to make you a minister and a witness both of the things which you have seen and of the things which I will yet reveal to you. **Acts 26:16**

Then God blessed them, and God said to them, "Be fruitful and multiply; fill the earth and subdue it; have dominion over the fish of the sea, over the birds of the air, and over every living thing that moves on the earth." **Genesis 1:28**

A PRAYER ABOUT PROMOTION

Holy God, I thank You in advance for my promotion, knowing that promotion comes only from You. As a child of the Most High God, I promise to work heartily for the Lord in whatever I do. I will be completely humble before the Lord, knowing that He will exalt me. My name will be made great so that I will be a blessing. Therefore, I have now been made alive with Christ and am seated with Him in the heavenly realms in Christ Jesus. So thank You Lord for the promotion both physically and spiritually, Amen.

And whatever you do, do it heartily, as to the Lord and not to men. **Colossians 3:23**

I will make you a great nation; I will bless you and make your name great; And you shall be a blessing. **Genesis 12:2**

And raised us up together, and made us sit together in the heavenly places in Christ Jesus. **Ephesians 2:6**

Carol Clarke Ministries

A PRAYER ABOUT INFERTILITY (BARRENNESS)

Faithful Lord, I know there is nothing impossible for my God! Like Sarah, I receive supernatural power to conceive, because I consider You faithful concerning Your promises. I will break forth in singing and cry aloud because I am no longer in a state of barrenness and hopelessness; I am confident through You, that the children of the barren one will be more than the children of her who is married. Therefore, I will commit my ways to the Lord, trusting in Him, knowing that You shall bring it to pass. Thank You Father, Amen.

By faith Sarah herself also received strength to conceive seed, and she bore a child when she was past the age, because she judged Him faithful who had promised. **Hebrews 11:11**

Commit your way to the Lord, Trust also in Him, And He shall bring it to pass. **Psalm 37:5**

"Sing, O barren, You who have not borne! Break forth into singing, and cry aloud, You who have not labored with child! For more are the children of the desolate than the children of the married woman," says the Lord. **Isaiah 54:1**

A PRAYER ABOUT VISION

Dear Lord, without vision, the people perish! Therefore, I will see potential in what others overlook because I have been entrusted with a global vision because my God is a global God. Therefore, I will write the vision and make it plain, that whoever reads it will run with it. Though it tarries, I will wait for it; because it will surely come. This is the prayer of my heart, Amen.

Then the Lord answered me and said: "Write the vision and make it plain on tablets, That he may run who reads it. For the vision is yet for an appointed time; But at the end it will speak, and it will not lie. Though it tarries, wait for it; Because it will surely come, It will not tarry". **Habakkuk 2:2-3**

Carol Clarke Ministries

A PRAYER ABOUT OVERCOMING GRIEF

Holy God, I bless Your Name, even in time of challenges, distress and grief. Father, through Your strength, I will overcome grief. I will not allow the fear of loss, or losses themselves, dictate my ability to relish the wonderful life that is rightfully mine. Although my flesh and my heart may fail, I am confident that God is the strength of my heart and my portion forever. Therefore, I will not let my heart be troubled, but my trust, hope and confidence remain in You, in Jesus Name, Amen.

My flesh and my heart fail; But God is the strength of my heart and my portion forever. **Psalm 73:26**

"Let not your heart be troubled; you believe in God, believe also in Me." **John 14:1**

A PRAYER ABOUT SELF-CONTROL

Dear Father, I place before You, the spirit of self-destruction that tries to dictate and control my life. I declare from this day forward that my life will be one of self-control and self-discipline. I will not run without an aim. I will not box as though I am just beating the air. However, I will discipline my body and make it enslaved to the Spirit that lives within me. Therefore, I will be strong in the Lord and the power of His might, putting on the whole armour of God so that I can stand against the schemes of the enemy.

Finally, my brethren, be strong in the Lord and in the power of His might. 11 Put on the whole armor of God, that you may be able to stand against the wiles of the devil. **Ephesians 6:10-11**

A PRAYER ABOUT UNDERSTANDING

Oh Lord, I will incline my ear unto wisdom and apply my heart to understanding the things of God. Father, I pray Your Word that declares that If I cry after knowledge and lift up my voice to understanding, then I find the knowledge of God; if I search for understanding as I would search for hidden treasure, I will understand the fear of the Lord. Holy Spirit, guide me in understanding the things of heaven; thank You Lord, Amen.

So that you incline your ear to wisdom, and apply your heart to understanding; Yes, if you cry out for discernment, and lift up your voice for understanding, If you seek her as silver, And search for her as for hidden treasures; Then you will understand the fear of the Lord, And find the knowledge of God. **Proverbs 2:2-5**

A PRAYER ABOUT PATIENCE

Dear Lord, I pray that You will teach me patience, as I recognise this is an area in my life that I struggle with. From today, I will strive to be completely humble and gentle; being patient, bearing with one another in love. Father clothe me with compassion, kindness, gentleness and patience. Just as You God gives endurance and encouragement, help me to be like-minded towards others in the same way according to Christ Jesus, Amen.

With all lowliness and gentleness, with longsuffering, bearing with one another in love. **Ephesians 4:2**

Therefore, as the elect of God, holy and beloved, put on tender mercies, kindness, humility, meekness, longsuffering. **Colossians 3:12**

Now may the God of patience and comfort grant you to be likeminded toward one another, according to Christ Jesus. **Romans 15:5**

A PRAYER ABOUT COMPASSION

Precious Father, at all times, I will demonstrate a heart of compassion, encouraging others and building them up. Lord, help me to highly esteem those who are over me in the Lord in love because of their work. Therefore, I walk in peace, encouraging the fainthearted, helping the weak, demonstrating patience to those I come in contact with. Lord, I know I cannot do this without Your divine Holy Spirit; thank You Lord, Amen.

Therefore comfort each other and edify one another, just as you also are doing. And we urge you, brethren, to recognize those who labor among you, and are over you in the Lord and admonish you and to esteem them very highly in love for their work's sake. Be at peace among yourselves. Now we exhort you, brethren, warn those who are unruly, comfort the fainthearted, uphold the weak, be patient with all. **1 Thessalonians 5:11-14**

A PRAYER ABOUT CAREER ACHIEVEMENT

Heavenly Father, I bless You for my career achievement in Jesus Name. I speak into the atmosphere that I will achieve all that is purposed for me. I will be successful in my career as You Lord continue to direct this area of my life. I am confident that I will achieve and accomplish much because Your Word reminds me of the promises that if I delight in You, You will give me the desires of my heart. Therefore, I commit my career achievements to You Lord, knowing that You have already established my plans.

Delight yourself also in the Lord, and He shall give you the desires of your heart. **Psalm 37:4**

Commit your works to the Lord, and your thoughts will be established. **Proverbs 16:3**

Carol Clarke Ministries

A PRAYER ABOUT OVERCOMING PAST FAILURES

Thank You Father – I praise You today because I have overcome my past failures. Lord life has been a challenge and admittedly, I have not always trusted in You as I should. So Father, I first ask for your forgiveness and I give You thanks for Your divine protection over my life. I declare that I have overcome past failures; I will forget the former things and not dwell on the past because God is doing a new thing. Therefore I am forgetting what is behind and reaching forward to those things which are ahead, I press toward the goal for the prize of the upward call of God in Christ Jesus, Amen.

Do not remember the former things, Nor consider the things of old. **Isaiah 43:18**

Brethren, I do not count myself to have [a]apprehended; but one thing I do, forgetting those things which are behind and reaching forward to those things which are ahead, I press toward the goal for the prize of the upward call of God in Christ Jesus. **Philippians 3:13-14**

A PRAYER ABOUT BETRAYAL

Dear loving Father, I am thankful because I am assured that You will never leave me or forsake me in times of difficulties, sickness or challenges because You have chosen me. Father, I know that You are always by my side; however, I feel betrayed by those who say they love and care for me but could not deal with the challenges of sickness against me. But Lord, will you help me to move on from those who have betrayed and hurt me during this time of injury/illness. You said Come to me, all who labour and are heavy laden, and I will give you rest. So, as I come to You, please will You heal my broken heart and bind up my wounds, in Jesus Name, Amen.

Be strong and of good courage, do not fear nor be afraid of them; for the Lord your God, He is the One who goes with you. He will not leave you nor forsake you. **Deuteronomy 31:6**

He heals the broken-hearted and binds up their wounds. **Psalm 147:3**

Come to Me, all you who labor and are heavy laden, and I will give you rest. **Matthew 11:28**

A PRAYER ABOUT JOB PROSPERITY

Oh Lord, I thank You for joy and despite my situation and circumstance, I shall forever shout for joy because You defend me. I put my trust in You and even though I am out of work right now, I know that I shall have job prosperity and therefore I shall rejoice because my trust, hope and confidence is in You. I love Your Name Lord, so I will be joyful in You and in all that You will do through me, Amen.

But let all those rejoice who put their trust in You; Let them ever shout for joy, because You defend them; Let those also who love Your name Be joyful in You. **Psalm 5:11**

A PRAYER FOR STRENGTH FOR THOSE IN DEBT

Heavenly Father, we pray for those who are imprisoned by an increasing burden of debts and cannot see a way out. Holy Spirit, You are an enabler and therefore, with You, it is possible for those who are bound by their debts to be set free in Jesus Name. Father, give every person hope and strength to tackle challenging situations and faith the size of a mustard seed. As they cry out to You, in their distress, will you hear their petition and give strength, as they put their hope and confidence in You, thank You Lord, Amen.

Therefore, if the Son makes you free, you shall be free indeed. **John 8:36**

So Jesus said to them, "Because of your unbelief; for assuredly, I say to you, if you have faith as a mustard seed, you will say to this mountain, 'Move from here to there,' and it will move; and nothing will be impossible for you. **Matthew 17:20**

A PRAYER OF STRENGTH FOR THOSE WHO ARE SICK

Our Father, we believe in the power of the blood of Jesus Christ and that You bore our pain and sickness on the cross. I have the assurance that You took the wounds for my transgressions; You were bruised because of my sins; Every stripe, You took on the cross means that I am healed. So, we thank you that our hope and trust for healing is in You. Sweet Saviour, by Your authority and power, will You bring divine healing, so that I can experience Your peace that surpasses all understanding; the peace that guards my heart and mind in Jesus Name – Thank You Father!

But He was wounded for our transgressions, He was bruised for our iniquities; The chastisement for our peace was upon Him, and by His stripes we are healed. **Isaiah 53:5**

And the peace of God, which surpasses all understanding, will guard your hearts and minds through Christ Jesus. **Philippians 4:7**

A PRAYER ABOUT FEELING UNLOVED

Dear Father, thank You that You are the God of comfort and love. It is through the death of Jesus Christ on the cross that the power of love was manifested for all mankind. So, please stretch out Your arms so that anyone who is feeling lonely or unloved right now, will feel and sense Your agape love. I know that Love never fails because Your Word reminds us that we must abide in faith, hope, love, but the greatest of these is love; thank You Lord, Amen.

And now abide faith, hope, love, these three; but the greatest of these is love. **1 Corinthians 13:13**

A PRAYER ABOUT THE HOMELESS

Heavenly Father, we thank you because Your Word says that because You love us, You gave your only begotten Son to die for us. So, we thank You that Your love extends to every ethnic group, all genders, race, colour and socio-economic classifications. Right now, we offer this prayer for the homeless. We pray that You will bless all men, women and children who may be without shelter across the globe. We pray for divine covering and blessing upon the homeless who have no one to take them in. Help me to respond to the cry of the poor because if I close my ears, I too will not be answered. Lord, flood the homeless with warmth, security and protection. Be their refuge, strength and present help in trouble. We commit this prayer to You, in Jesus Name. Amen!

God is our refuge and strength, a very present help in trouble. **Psalm 46:1**

Whoever closes his ear to the cry of the poor will himself call out and not be answered. **Proverbs 21:13**

A PRAYER ABOUT THE LOST

Dear Lord, I recognise that I am lost in this evil world and I feel far from You. But Father, I pray that You forgive me for the things that I have knowingly and unknowingly done that displeases You. Lord I thank You because if I confess my sins, in Your faithfulness and just nature, You wholeheartedly are able to forgive me and cleanse me from all unrighteousness. I love You Father and thank You that I do not have to remain in my lost state because You gave Your Son so that we would not perish, but have eternal life; thank You Holy One, Amen.

If we confess our sins, He is faithful and just to forgive us our sins and to cleanse us from all unrighteousness. **1 John 1:9**

For God so loved the world that He gave His only begotten Son, that whoever believes in Him should not perish but have everlasting life. **John 3:16**

A PRAYER ABOUT MARRIAGE

Heavenly Father, we thank You for your love towards us and the command You have given, to love You and each other. I pray that every marriage will be selfless and centred on You. Let marriages reflect a Godly relationship, laying aside infidelity, adultery, lust and pride. Father help every married couple to unite in their thoughts, respecting the fact that their way of thinking may differ from each other. Let couples spend time loving one another from their hearts, in the same way You have loved us, Amen.

Teacher, which is the great commandment in the law?" Jesus said to him, "'You shall love the Lord your God with all your heart, with all your soul, and with all your mind.' This is the first and great commandment. And the second is like it: 'You shall love your neighbor as yourself.' **Matthew 22:36-39**

Therefore, be imitators of God as dear children. And walk in love, as Christ also has loved us and given Himself for us, an offering and a sacrifice to God for a sweet-smelling aroma. **Ephesians 5:1-2**

A PRAYER ABOUT DEALING WITH OVEREATING

Heavenly Father, thank You for reminding us to pray that we may not enter into temptation. I pray Lord that I will not sin against my body by overeating, because my body is the temple of the Holy Spirit who is in me. I recognise the power of prayer over my weight gain and I ask that You break down those strongholds in my life as I war against the enemy, through the blood of Jesus Christ. I pray that my will shall always be aligned to Your agenda because I know that I am not my own; thank You Lord, Amen.

Watch and pray, lest you enter into temptation. The spirit indeed is willing, but the flesh is weak." **Matthew 26:41**

Do you not know that your body is the temple of the Holy Spirit who is in you, whom you have from God, and you are not your own? **1 Corinthians 6:19**

A PRAYER ABOUT PEACE

Dear Lord, thank you for Your peace that surpasses all understanding. I thank You that Your Word teaches me to say, Peace, be still! Just as Christ rebuked the wind and the sea, I thank You that You have given me the power and the authority to silence every turmoil and earthquake in my life in Jesus Name. I will choose not to be anxious about anything because I have the assurance that You will keep me in perfect peace as my mind stays on You; thank You Jehovah Shalom (Lord is peace), In Jesus Name.

And the peace of God, which surpasses all understanding, will guard your hearts and minds through Christ Jesus. **Philippians 4:7**

Then He arose and rebuked the wind, and said to the sea, "Peace,[a] be still!" And the wind ceased and there was a great calm. **Mark 4:39**

You will keep him in perfect peace, Whose mind is stayed on You, Because he trusts in You. **Isaiah 26:3**

A PRAYER ABOUT ENDURANCE

Majestic God, I thank You that through You, I can accomplish all that I set out to complete. I pray that You will help me to walk in determination, steadfastness and endurance. Give me the strength to finish what I have started and endure to the end, just as Christ endured the cross. Father, I trust in Your Word, and I will put aside every weight, and the sin which so easily ensnares me, and I will run with endurance the race that is set before me; this I pray, in Jesus Name.

Therefore we also, since we are surrounded by so great a cloud of witnesses, let us lay aside every weight, and the sin which so easily ensnares us, and let us run with endurance the race that is set before us.
Hebrews 12:1

A PRAYER ABOUT LOVE

Lord Jesus, I thank You and honour You for the love you gave when you died on the cross. Father, I ask that you teach me to love, just as You demonstrate the love of The Father who is in heaven. Help me to love, because love covers a multitude of sins. Love is also patient, kind and does not envy. Love is not jealous or boastful or proud. Therefore, because Christ first loved me, I walk in love keeping no record of wrong and never losing faith, Amen.

For God so loved the world that He gave His only begotten Son, that whoever believes in Him should not perish but have everlasting life. **John 3:16**

Love suffers long and is kind; love does not envy; love does not parade itself, is not puffed up; does not behave rudely, does not seek its own, is not provoked, thinks no evil; does not rejoice in iniquity, but rejoices in the truth; bears all things, believes all things, hopes all things, endures all things. Love never fails. But whether there are prophecies, they will fail; whether there are tongues, they will cease; whether there is knowledge, it will vanish away. **1 Corinthians 13:4-8**

And above all things have fervent love for one another, for "love will cover a multitude of sins." **1 Peter 4:8**

A PRAYER ABOUT KNIFE CRIME ADDICTS

Dear Lord, we bless You that Your Word reminds us that we are sinners saved by Grace. We pray for those families who have lost loved ones to knife crime addicts. We ask that Your Holy Spirit will intervene in their hearts and that You Lord, will transform their character. God, we acknowledge that the wages of sin is death, but the free gift of God is eternal Life in Christ Jesus our Lord. As we pray this prayer, please bring consolation and peace in the midst of grief. We ask that You grant the free gift of Eternal Life to 'knife crime addicts' in Jesus Name. Help them to surrender their hearts to You, so they can be with You eternally, Amen.

For the wages of sin is death, but the gift of God is eternal life in Christ Jesus our Lord. **Romans 6:23**

A PRAYER ABOUT GOVERNMENT

Dear God, I pray that in Your mercy, You will hear the cry of the saints for our government and nation during this time of chaos and uncertainty. Lord, we pray against the spirit of disunity, doubt, fear and isolation amongst government leaders and politicians. Pour out the spirit of cooperation, unity and collaboration, upon leaders of this country, so that they will be governed by Your Holy Spirit because the lack of counsel a nation falls, but victory is won through many advisers. Lord, we declare that even in such uncertainty, You are our shield and strength, in whom we trust, Amen.

Where there is no counsel, the people fall; But in the multitude of counselors there is safety. **Proverbs 11:14**

A PRAYER ABOUT FINANCIAL MIRACLE

Eternal God, Your Word says that I should not worry about what I shall eat, or what I shall drink or what I shall wear. Therefore, I know that I shouldn't worry about my finances. For the pagans chase after these things, and You, my heavenly Father knows that I need them. Lord, You know that I need a financial miracle right now. You know that I need an overflow of money, let the drought that currently occupies my bank account be gone in Jesus Name, Amen.

"Therefore, do not worry, saying, 'What shall we eat?' or 'What shall we drink?' or 'What shall we wear?' 32 For after all these things the Gentiles seek. For your heavenly Father knows that you need all these things. **Matthew 6:31-32**

Carol Clarke Ministries

A PRAYER ABOUT HEALING FROM CANCER

Lord, You alone are God, all inferior gods are incomparable to You - Yahweh. It is You who controls events and has power over both death and life. You who can inflict wounds and heal, and from Your hand, no one can deliver. My cancer is in Your hands; my healing is in Your hands; I pray that You have Your divine way in my life. I pray for Your divine hand to rest upon my health; thank You Lord for divine healing from cancer, in Jesus Name, Amen.

Now see that I, even I, am He, And there is no God besides Me; I kill and I make alive; I wound and I heal; Nor is there any who can deliver from My hand. **Deuteronomy 32:39**

A PRAYER FOR GOOD WEATHER

Mighty Warrior, I praise You because You are a God of true power. When You utter Your voice, there is a tumult of waters in the heavens, and You cause the clouds to ascend from the end of the earth! I pray that You order creation to bless us, so that we may enjoy nature and good weather. I declare that we will take advantage of the good weather that You are about to bless us with, Amen.

When He utters His voice, There is a multitude of waters in the heavens: And He causes the vapors to ascend from the ends of the earth. He makes lightning for the rain, He brings the wind out of His treasuries. **Jeremiah 10:13**

Carol Clarke Ministries

A PRAYER ABOUT COURT VICTORY

Righteous Saviour, I trust in You for my protection. As I battle in court right now, it is not the lawyers that I put my trust in, nor is it the judge, but my trust is in You. My court victory is in Your hands, and I know that I will have the victory because You have never failed me. I pray that You hear my cries, and I thank You in advance for helping me win this battle, Amen.

In the Lord I put my trust... **Psalm 11:1**

Trust in Him at all times, you people Pour out your heart before Him; God is a refuge for us. **Psalm 62:8**

A PRAYER WHEN IN FEAR

Our Father who art in heaven, hallowed be Your Name. I acknowledge who You are; You are Holy and You are Worthy. You are Mighty and all powerful. Therefore, because you have dominion over creation and You breathed Your own breath in me, I have been created in your image. If I have been created by You who is all powerful, I will not fear, because you are with me and Your Holy Spirit is inside of me. Therefore, I will not be dismayed because You are my God. So thank you for your strength, help and guidance; Thank You Father for upholding me with Your righteous right hand, Amen.

Fear not, for I am with you; Be not dismayed, for I am your God. I will strengthen you, Yes, I will help you, I will uphold you with My righteous right hand. **Isaiah 41:10**

Carol Clarke Ministries

A PRAYER ABOUT EMOTIONAL STABILITY

Heavenly Father thank You for Your love and compassion towards me. Lord, I have felt like giving up because of my emotional instability, but Lord, I thank you for Your blessings upon me. I declare that I am restored spiritually, physically and emotionally through the Power of Jesus Christ. Father, I know that You have heard my cry, and You have made me perfect and stablished. You have strengthened and settled me. So, Father, I rededicate myself totally to You, surrendering my will to Your Will, my ways to Your ways and my thoughts to Your thoughts in Jesus Name Amen.

"For My thoughts are not your thoughts, Nor are your ways My ways," says the Lord. **Isaiah 55:8**

But may the God of all grace, who called us to His eternal glory by Christ Jesus, after you have suffered a while, perfect, establish, strengthen, and settle you. **1 Peter 5:10**

A PRAYER ABOUT SURGERY

May the Lord strengthen my body, as I lie in weight for surgery. May You grant me supernatural protection and divine healing that comes only from Your throne. Lord, if it is Your will, take the place of the surgeon as I undergo this operation; I ask that You conduct a supernatural procedure because You are the great physician who I trust wholeheartedly. Lord, I exercise faith in Your Word, knowing that Your Will shall be done in this situation because you give strength to the weary and increase power to the weak; thank You Lord, Amen.

He gives power to the weak, and to those who have no might He increases strength. **Isaiah 40:29**

A PRAYER ABOUT BAD DREAMS

Holy God, I pray against my bad dreams right now. I proclaim that whatever I bind on earth shall be bound in heaven, and whatever I loose on earth shall be loosed in heaven. I bind up the attacks that the adversary has had on my sleep in Jesus' Name. I declare sweet, God-given dreams when I lay my head to rest. I declare that the plans that the enemy has on my sleep and over my life be destroyed, Amen.

Assuredly, I say to you, "whatever you bind on earth will be bound in heaven, and whatever you loose on earth will be loosed in heaven."
Matthew 18:18

A PRAYER ABOUT KNIFE CRIME VICTIMS

Dear Father, we present before You those who are victims of knife crime. We ask that You touch their hearts. Lord, heal their brokenness and help them not to think and reflect on the violence, but help them to turn towards peace in their hearts. So, Heavenly Father, for every knife crime victim, we ask that You bless them and keep them; make Your face shine upon them and be gracious to them; Father turn your face towards them and give them peace in the midst of turmoil, this we pray, Amen.

"The Lord bless you and keep you; The Lord make His face shine upon you, and be gracious to you; The Lord [a]lift up His countenance upon you, and give you peace." **Numbers 6:24-26**

Carol Clarke Ministries

A PRAYER ABOUT PRESSURES AT WORK

Dear Lord, Almighty God, I cry out to You because I am experiencing so much pressure at work. I ask for your help and divine strength to get through each day. Father, I can no longer bear the pressure of work commitments, as it is affecting my health. Lord help me to not be a slave to masters of various organisations, but to be a slave to You. So, I commit this job totally to You because You said in Your Word that I must cast all my cares on You because You care for me. Lord, please give me Your wisdom I pray, Amen.

Casting all your care upon Him, for He cares for you. **1 Peter 5:7**

A PRAYER ABOUT IDENTITY

Precious Father, I declare that I am created in Your image; the image of God. Therefore, I will not question my identity because Your Word reminds me that I am fearfully and wonderfully made. Society at times aims to place people in a 'pigeon hole' based on personal traits and characteristics. But Holy God, I declare that I will not fit into what others say about me, but I will mount up on wings like eagles; I will run and not be weary despite peers around me losing their identity; thank You Lord; creator of the universe, Amen.

I will praise You, for I am fearfully and wonderfully made; Marvelous are Your works, and that my soul knows very well. **Psalm 139:14**

But those who wait on the Lord shall renew their strength; they shall mount up with wings like eagles, they shall run and not be weary, they shall walk and not faint. **Isaiah 40:31**

A PRAYER ABOUT DEALING WITH CONFRONTATION

Holy Spirit, I thank You for allowing me to face confrontational situations in my life. Often times, these are not pleasant, but Lord teach me how to deal with confrontations in a Godly way. God, like King Asa, I am faced with a great multitude that rises against me. But God I know there is no one besides You to help in dealing with confrontation. Lord, help me because I trust in You. I pray the prayer of Jehoshaphat, that Lord I know not what to do, but in every confrontational situation, my eyes will remain on You, Amen.

And Asa cried out to the Lord his God, and said, "Lord, it is nothing for You to help, whether with many or with those who have no power; help us, O Lord our God, for we rest on You, and in Your name we go against this multitude. O Lord, You are our God; do not let man prevail against You!" **2 Chronicles 14:11**

O our God, will You not judge them? For we have no power against this great multitude that is coming against us; nor do we know what to do, but our eyes are upon You." **2 Chronicles 20:12**

A PRAYER ABOUT CHEMOTHERAPY PATIENTS

Blessed God, You have commanded me to be strong and courageous. It's hard because with chemotherapy, I don't know if it will work; neither do the doctors know for certain. But Lord, You know all things. Therefore, I find comfort in knowing that You are in control and You are not surprised by anything. I will not be terrified because You go with me; You will never leave me nor forsake me, Amen.

Be strong and of good courage, do not fear nor be afraid of them; for the Lord your God, He is the One who goes with you. He will not leave you nor forsake you." **Deuteronomy 31:6**

A PRAYER ABOUT FORGIVING YOURSELF

Dear Lord, I feel oppressed by my past and my sins. The devil wants me to remain in my guilt and shame instead of embracing Your love. Father, help me to be renewed in my thinking, according to Your Word. Your Word also reminds me that nothing can separate me from Your love; allow me to remember this whenever my past is brought to the forefront of my thoughts. Through Your love, I declare freedom from the guilt and pain of my past, Amen.

And be renewed in the spirit of your mind… nor give place to the devil. **Ephesians 4:23, 27**

Who shall separate us from the love of Christ? Shall tribulation, or distress, or persecution, or famine, or nakedness, or peril, or sword? **Romans 8:35**

A PRAYER ABOUT RACIAL HEALING

Dear Lord, I pray for generations that have been affected by racial hate and families that have felt oppressed because they have been marginalised due to the colour of their skin. Let the oppressed realise that they are royalty in Your eyes. Help them to realise that whom the Son sets free is free indeed. Let the broken-hearted be healed by Your love. Let racial abuse be non-existent in our cities and nations, rather than the norm. Let the weak rise up and be strengthened by You, this Lord we ask, Amen.

But you are a chosen generation, a royal priesthood, a holy nation, His own special people, that you may proclaim the praises of Him who called you out of darkness into His marvelous light. **1 Peter 2: 9**

He gives power to the weak, and to those who have no might He increases strength. But those who wait on the Lord shall renew their strength; they shall mount up with wings like eagles, they shall run and not be weary, they shall walk and not faint. **Isaiah 40:29, 31**

Carol Clarke Ministries

A PRAYER ABOUT SUICIDAL THOUGHTS

Dear Father, suicide is often seen as a taboo topic, that is never discussed or talked about, but Lord, in my season of depression, emptiness and loneliness, suicide appears to be the only solution. But Father, I pray for Your help and protection over me; please pull me out of the enemies snare because Your Word reminds me that the devil comes to steal, kill and destroy, but You Lord have come to give life in abundance. So, Lord please do not let my life be snuffed out but help me to see beyond the darkness that often surrounds me; thank You Jesus, Amen.

The thief does not come except to steal, and to kill, and to destroy. I have come that they may have life, and that they may have it more abundantly. **John 10:10**

A PRAYER ABOUT DECISION MAKING

Oh Lord of Host, I thank You that I do not have to make decisions by myself. But oftentimes, I tend to make my own decisions without consulting You. Please forgive me Father and I pray that as I make plans, You God will direct my actions. Father, I will call to You because You promised to reveal unsearchable things that I did not know. So Father, from this day forward, I commit to every decision making be centred on God, Amen.

A man's heart plans his way, But the Lord directs his steps. **Proverbs 16:9**

Call to Me, and I will answer you, and show you great and [a]mighty things, which you do not know.' **Jeremiah 33:3**

Carol Clarke Ministries

A PRAYER ABOUT MENTAL ILLNESS

Dear Loving God, I come before You today to pray for those who are challenged by condition of mental illness. I also pray for divine strength for those who offer care to those with such afflictions. Have mercy upon them Oh God. I pray that the spirit of confusion and mental impairment be gone in Jesus Name. We take a stand against depression, anxiety, dementia, schizophrenia and any other mental illnesses in Jesus Name because Your Word says that who the Son sets free is free indeed. Lord free those who are under the bondage of mental illness in Jesus Name; it is not of You, so we declare the Victory in the Name of the Father, The Son and The Holy Spirit, Amen.

Therefore if the Son makes you free, you shall be free indeed. **John 8:36**

A PRAYER ABOUT FINDING A LOVE RELATIONSHIP

Lord of Host, may I find a love relationship with someone who I can share my life with. May you give me the desires of my heart because you know me and you know my thoughts from afar. So Father, I approach You in this prayer and ask that You will bring my expected life partner into my life because it is not good for a man or woman to be alone. May you grant me with the person You have chosen to be my love and friend. Amen.

Delight yourself also in the Lord, and He shall give you the desires of your heart. **Psalm 37:4**

You know my sitting down and my rising up; You understand my thought afar off. **Psalm 139:2**

And the Lord God said, "It is not good that man should be alone; I will make him a helper comparable to him." **Genesis 2:18**

Carol Clarke Ministries

A PRAYER ABOUT NEWBORN BABIES

Awesome God, I thank You for my baby who lays in my arms because he/she is a blessing! I also thank You for entrusting me with being a parent, a duty which I do not take for granted nor do I take lightly. I pray that I start my child off in the way that they should go, so that even when they become older, what I have taught will not be forgotten or ignored. I pray that my child remains rooted in You and stays on the paths that You have chosen for their life when he/she sleeps and when he/she is awake, Amen.

Train up a child in the way he should go, and when he is old he will not depart from it. **Proverbs 22:6**

A PRAYER ABOUT A SON AND DAUGHTER

Dear Heavenly Father, how majestic is Your Name in all the earth. I pray for my son/daughter and Your protection over their life. Thank You for the love you have given me to love, guide and teach them. May You help me to release my son/daughter to You, so that you can fulfil the desires you have for their lives. Help them to live as sons and daughters of God by faith in Christ Jesus. I pray that these blessings shall cover my son/daughter, by the power of your Holy Spirit; thank You Lord, Amen.

For you are all sons of God through faith in Christ Jesus.
Galatians 3:26

Carol Clarke Ministries

A PRAYER ABOUT GRIEF AND COMFORT

Dear Lord, the grief I feel right now is unbearable. I understand that You know how I feel because You created me and I know that You care for me. I cast all of my sadness on You so that I can feel whole again. Please take away the pain so that I can be filled with peace. Make my heart whole so that I can feel joy again. Lord, I love You and thank You for being with me during this difficult period of my life, Amen.

Casting all your care upon Him, for He cares for you. **1 Peter 5:7**

A PRAYER ABOUT RENEWAL OF YOUTH

Holy God, I thank You because Your Word reminds me that I am a new creation in Christ. I have put on my new self which is being renewed in knowledge after the image of God. I bless You for the renewal of youth, despite negative words spoken over them by society. I shall not yield to these negative words, but I receive by faith Your divine life to flow in me, giving strength and power to youth. I confidently hope in the Lord, knowing that my strength shall be renewed; Lord, I bless You because I will soar on wings like eagles; I will run and not grow weary; I will walk and not be faint; this is my prayer. Amen.

And have put on the new man who is renewed in knowledge according to the image of Him who created him. **Colossians 3:10**

He gives power to the weak, and to those who have no might He increases strength. Even the youths shall faint and be weary, and the young men shall utterly fall, but those who wait on the Lord shall renew their strength; they shall mount up with wings like eagles, they shall run and not be weary, they shall walk and not faint. **Isaiah 40:29-31**

Therefore, if anyone is in Christ, he is a new creation; old things have passed away; behold, all things have become new. **2 Corinthians 5:17**

A PRAYER ABOUT LONGEVITY

Righteous Father, I thank You for this season of my life. I declare that in this season, I will endure to the end. Teach me Lord, to love life and to see good days, as You see them. Help me Lord, to honour my father and mother (both natural and spiritual), so that my days may be prolonged in the land which You Lord God have given me. Like Moses, my eyes will not dim and my natural vigour will not diminish. Therefore, I rest and wait patiently for You, in Jesus Name, I pray, Amen.

Honor your father and your mother, that your days may be long upon the land which the Lord your God is giving you. **Exodus 20:12**

Moses was one hundred and twenty years old when he died. His eyes were not dim nor his natural vigor diminished. **Deuteronomy 34:7**

A PRAYER ABOUT COMMUNITY INVOLVEMENT

Dear Lord, I thank You for who You are, and I thank You for this community. I pray that You will have Your divine way within the hearts of Your people so that they become more willing to help those around them. I pray that this community flourishes and that every individual becomes more involved because Your Word says that two are better than one; because they have a good reward for their labour; this is the prayer of our heart, Amen.

Two are better than one, because they have a good reward for their labor. **Ecclesiastes 4:9**

A PRAYER ABOUT SPEAKING IN TONGUES

Dear Father, I thank You for the gift of speaking in tongues. I recognise that this heavenly language comes directly from the Father through Jesus Christ. Lord, I ask for Your Holy Spirit to intercede on my behalf because He who searches the hearts knows what the mind of the spirit is, according to the will of God. Lord through Your power and authority; teach me to speak as the Holy Spirit gives utterance, uttering mysteries by the Spirit. Father, help me to flow in the Spirit, building up faith by praying in the Holy Spirit as You Father bids me. Thank You Lord, Amen.

Now He who searches the hearts knows what the mind of the Spirit is, because He makes intercession for the saints according to the will of God. **Romans 8:27**

But you, beloved, building yourselves up on your most holy faith, praying in the Holy Spirit. **Jude 1:20**

A PRAYER ABOUT FAITH

Heavenly Father, You said in Your Word that "faith is the substance of things hoped for, the evidence of things not seen". As faith cannot be seen, I choose to walk by faith and not by sight, by the leading of Your Holy Spirit. Through faith, I will *see* the invisible, *believe* the unbelievable and *receive* the impossible. Even if my faith is as small as a mustard seed, I can speak to the mountain: 'move from here to there', and it will move. Therefore, I live by faith in the Son of God, who loved me and gave himself for me, Amen.

Now faith is the substance of things hoped for, the evidence of things not seen. **Hebrews 11:1**

So Jesus said to them, "Because of your unbelief; for assuredly, I say to you, if you have faith as a mustard seed, you will say to this mountain, 'Move from here to there,' and it will move; and nothing will be impossible for you. **Matthew 17:20**

I have been crucified with Christ; it is no longer I who live, but Christ lives in me; and the life which I now live in the flesh I live by faith in the Son of God, who loved me and gave Himself for me. **Galatians 2:20**

Carol Clarke Ministries

A PRAYER ABOUT CHURCH LEADERSHIP

Dear Father, we pray for the leadership of our church and declare that no weapon formed shall prosper. We pray that you will grant our leaders with the spirit of Solomon; give them wisdom, knowledge and understanding so that they may lead by the directing of the Holy Spirit and in line with the will and purpose of God. Father we ask that the spirit of counsel and anointing will rest upon the leadership of our church so that they will preach the gospel of Jesus Christ with clarity, not compromising 'truth' in Christ Jesus our Lord, Amen.

No weapon formed against you shall prosper, and every tongue which rises against you in judgment You shall condemn. This is the heritage of the servants of the LORD, and their righteousness is from Me," Says the LORD. **Isaiah 54:17**

Now give me wisdom and knowledge, that I may go out and come in before this people; for who can judge this great people of Yours? **2 Chronicles 1:10**

A PRAYER ABOUT THE BODY OF CHRIST

Heavenly Father, we approach you in total love and adoration. We magnify and exalt Your Holy Name. As the Body of Christ, we give you all the honour in which you deserve. So, Father help us to unite as one because Your Word reminds us that 'where two or three gather together touching anything concerning You, You are there in the midst'. Bless us Lord and help us find harmony with each other, as we work together for Your Kingdom, Amen.

"For where two or three are gathered together in My name, I am there in the midst of them." **Matthew 18:20**

Carol Clarke Ministries

A PRAYER ABOUT BOLDNESS TO PROCLAIM THE GOSPEL

Our Father Who art in Heaven, Hallowed be Your Name in all the earth in which You rule and have dominion. We pray that the gospel of Jesus Christ will be proclaimed in all the earth with boldness, clarity and without fear. Thank You for reminding us that, You have not given us the spirit of fear but of power and love and of a sound mind. Therefore, we receive by faith, the power of God to preach the gospel. We thank Him for supernatural strength and grace to preach the Word of God, that transforms the heart of sinners to true repentance. Father, give us boldness, faith, wisdom and understanding through the power of the Holy Spirit to "root out, pull down, destroy, throw down, build and plant" in Jesus Name.

See, I have this day set you over the nations and over the kingdoms, To root out and to pull down, To destroy and to throw down, To build and to plant." **Jeremiah 1:10**

For God has not given us a spirit of fear, but of power and of love and of a sound mind. **Timothy 1:7**

A PRAYER ABOUT PASTORS

Heavenly Father, as a pastor it is easy to go down the path of self-doubt. I pray against any doubts that I have in myself or in You because before I was formed in the womb, You knew me! Therefore when I was born I was set apart; You appointed me as a prophet to the nations. Lord, I rejoice in Your word because Your word never fails nor lies. My ministry was ordained by You, therefore I know that I should be doing this and that I can do this because it is in line with the will that You have for my life. Father, whenever I doubt, I pray that I remember that You have called me and that You have a great plan for my life and for my ministry, Amen.

Before I formed you in the womb I knew you; Before you were born I sanctified you; I ordained you a prophet to the nations." **Jeremiah 1:5**

Carol Clarke Ministries

A PRAYER ABOUT ACTIVATING YOUR SPIRITUAL GIFT

Thank You Lord, for the spiritual gifts you have given me. I thank You for those gifts that have not yet been revealed to me – Father, I trust and wait on Your timing. I declare that I will operate in the spiritual gifts given to me by the Holy Spirit. I will make every effort to pursue and activate the gift that wants to lay dormant on the inside of me. Therefore, I will use whatever gift I have received to serve others, as a faithful steward of God's grace and will fan into flames the spiritual gift God has given, Amen.

As each one has received a gift, minister it to one another, as good stewards of the manifold grace of God. **1 Peter 4:10**

Therefore, I remind you to stir up the gift of God which is in you through the laying on of my hands. **2 Timothy 1:6**

A PRAYER ABOUT WISDOM

Heavenly Father, thank You for wisdom, knowledge and understanding that comes from You. I bless You Lord because this wisdom is pure, then peaceable, gentle and full of mercy and good fruits. Father, I pray that I shall not be wise in my own eyes, but I will walk in the wisdom, knowledge and happiness given by You. I will therefore operate in the pure wisdom that comes from heaven, and I shall utter words of wisdom speaking only what is just. Help me to not lack wisdom because You God give generously without finding fault; thank You Father, Amen.

Do not be wise in your own eyes; Fear the Lord and depart from evil. **Proverbs 3:7**

But the wisdom that is from above is first pure, then peaceable, gentle, willing to yield, full of mercy and good fruits, without partiality and without hypocrisy. **James 3:17**

If any of you lacks wisdom, let him ask of God, who gives to all liberally and without reproach, and it will be given to him. **James 1:5**

A PRAYER FOR CHILDREN TO SAY

Dear Father, I pray that You help me be the light in a world of darkness. Please help me understand and believe that whilst You are in me, I am greater than anything in and of the world. Help me be strong and turn away from the false pleasures the world has to offer. I pray that I will not be overcome by evil, but I will overcome evil with good. Father let Your goodness be evidence of true greatness, this I pray, Amen.

You are of God, little children, and have overcome them, because He who is in you is greater than he who is in the world. **1 John 4:4**

Do not be overcome by evil, but overcome evil with good. **Romans 12:21**

A PRAYER ABOUT DISCERNMENT

Almighty God, Thank You for the spirit of discernment that works within me. Lord, I refuse to believe every spirit, because Your Word reminds me to test the spirits as to whether they are of God. I am aware that every spirit that confesses not, that Jesus Christ is come in the flesh, is not of God, but is the spirit of the antichrist. I am a child of God and I have overcome them, because greater is He that is in me, than he that is in the world. So, Lord, I pray that You will continue to give me the gift of discernment so that I will continue to be led by the spirit of truth, casting out the spirit of error, Amen.

Beloved, do not believe every spirit, but test the spirits, whether they are of God; because many false prophets have gone out into the world. By this you know the Spirit of God: Every spirit that confesses that Jesus Christ has come in the flesh is of God, and every spirit that does not confess that Jesus Christ has come in the flesh is not of God. And this is the spirit of the Antichrist, which you have heard was coming, and is now already in the world. You are of God, little children, and have overcome them, because He who is in you is greater than he who is in the world. They are of the world. Therefore, they speak as of the world, and the world hears them. We are of God. He who knows God hears us; he who is not of God does not hear us. By this we know the spirit of truth and the spirit of error.
1 John 4:1-6

Carol Clarke Ministries

A PRAYER ABOUT CHRISTIAN VALUES

Our Father, we thank You because of who you are. We thank You for giving us clear guidance of the Christian values that we should portray in our own lives each and every day. Help us to be more like You; help us to be clothed in your image. Father we ask that we continue to exercise our Faith in You; Help us to have hope despite the circumstances. Father, we Love You with an agape love and just as You loved and served others, help us to also serve others with true humility so that the world can experience joy, justice and kindness in Jesus Name, Amen.

… and as we have borne the image of the man of dust, we shall also bear the image of the heavenly Man. **1 Corinthians 15:49**

A PRAYER ABOUT THE HOLY SPIRIT

Righteous and Mighty God, I give You thanks for the power of the Holy Spirit that dwells and lives within me. It is because of the triune God (Father, Son and Holy Spirit) that I can live and walk by the Holy Spirit. Father, even though the devil is walking around like a roaring lion, seeking who he can devour, I pray earnestly that Your Holy Spirit will continuously abide in me as I abide in You. You are my helper, teaching me to observe all things. So, I thank You for the power of the Holy Spirit that has come upon me to be a witness to the end of the earth, Amen.

But the Helper, the Holy Spirit, whom the Father will send in My name, He will teach you all things, and bring to your remembrance all things that I said to you. **John 14:26**

But you shall receive power when the Holy Spirit has come upon you; and you shall be witnesses to Me in Jerusalem, and in all Judea and Samaria, and to the end of the earth." **Acts 1:8**

Be sober, be vigilant; because your adversary the devil walks about like a roaring lion, seeking whom he may devour. **1 Peter 5:8**

Carol Clarke Ministries

A PRAYER ABOUT COMMITTING PLANS TO GOD

Dear Father, thank You that You have created me in your image. I bless you because you have given me a vision and purpose that must be fulfilled here on earth. I admit that I do not always seek You first in planning and doing the things that You have place in my heart, but Father, as of today, I commit my vision to You. You are the creator of my ideas; You are the driver of my vision, so I invite You into the whole process in Jesus Name. Please remove the things that are not of You and replace them with Your vision. Help me to be led by Your divine inspiration; I wait on Your timing because Your ways are always perfect. Your Word says that if I commit my works to You, my plans will be achieved. So, Father, I will delight myself in You because You said You will give me the desires of my heart. Thank You Father, Amen.

As for God, His way is perfect; The word of the Lord is proven; He is a shield to all who trust in Him. **Psalm 18:30**

To everything there is a season, A time for every purpose under heaven. **Ecclesiastes 3**

Delight yourself also in the Lord, And He shall give you the desires of your heart. **Psalm 37:4**

A PRAYER ABOUT MONEY AND STEWARDSHIP

Our Father, who art in heaven, hallowed be Your Name. I give You thanks that You provide all resources according to Your purpose and will for our lives. Lord, our society wants us to crave materialistic things, regardless of whether we have the money or not to satisfy our purchasing desires. But Lord, I pray that I will not allow my economic status to dictate who I am in You. Give me wisdom Father, to use money that You have given sensibly. Help me to give willing and generously for the Glory of Your Name, Amen.

For where your treasure is, there your heart will be also. **Matthew 6:21**

Carol Clarke Ministries

A PRAYER ABOUT THANKING GOD IN ADVANCE

Dear Lord, I thank You in advance because I know that I can do all things through You. It is You who strengthens me and You are my greatest weapon against the adversary. Therefore, I will prosper and I will be of good cheer because You have overcome the world. For this reason, I bless You for what You will do through me in the future. Lord I lean not on myself and I trust solely in You, Amen.

These things I have spoken to you, that in Me you may have peace. In the world you will have tribulation; but be of good cheer, I have overcome the world." **John 16:33**

I can do all things through Christ who strengthens me. **Philippians 4:13**

"No weapon formed against you shall prosper, and every tongue which rises against you in judgment You shall condemn. This is the heritage of the servants of the Lord, and their righteousness is from Me" Says the Lord. **Isaiah 54:17**

A PRAYER ABOUT SALVATION

Oh Lord, I bless Your Name for the promises of eternal life. I thank You that You have given me the opportunity to be rescued from sin. So right now, "I declare that nothing shall be able to separate me from God". Even though the enemy roams the earth, seeking one to devour, through Your Holy Spirit, I am convinced that neither death nor life, nor demons can separate me from Your Love that is in Christ Jesus; thank You Father for Salvation, Amen.

For I am persuaded that neither death nor life, nor angels nor principalities nor powers, nor things present nor things to come, nor height nor depth, nor any other created thing, shall be able to separate us from the love of God which is in Christ Jesus our Lord.
Romans 8:38-39

A PRAYER ABOUT BLESSINGS

Lord Jesus, I know that I am blessed with the blessings of God. Your Word says that I am a chosen generation, a royal priesthood, a holy nation, a peculiar people. Therefore, as a child of The Highest God, I receive every good and perfect gift from above. I lack nothing because You are my shepherd. Therefore, because I am blessed, goodness and love will follow me all the days of my life; thank You Lord, Amen.

Every good gift and every perfect gift is from above, and comes down from the Father of lights, with whom there is no variation or shadow of turning. **James 1:17**

The Lord is my shepherd; I shall not want. Surely goodness and mercy shall follow me All the days of my life; And I will dwell in the house of the Lord Forever. **Psalm 23:1, 6**

But you are a chosen generation, a royal priesthood, a holy nation, His own special people, that you may proclaim the praises of Him who called you out of darkness into His marvelous light. **1 Peter 2:9**

A PRAYER ABOUT DYING WITHOUT JESUS

Dear Jesus, You are the way, truth and life and no one can come to the Father except through You. It is Your Word that reminds us to repent and that we must confess our sins in order to receive Your mercy. Without accepting You into my life as my personal saviour, I am condemned to eternal damnation. Therefore, if I do not confess that Jesus is Lord and believe that God raised Him from death; when I die, I will not be saved. I shall then become separated from Christ Jesus… having no hope and being without God. So Father, I am sorry for committing sins, which have separated me from You. I ask for forgiveness in Jesus Name and declare that I want to turn away from my sinful past to accept eternal life rather than eternal punishment through Jesus Christ our Lord. I invite You Father, to be Lord over my life. I ask that You help me to exercise faith in You because it is by my faith that I am put right with God; it is by my confession that I am saved. So, please send Your Holy Spirit to bring correction so that I may obey You; this I ask, in Jesus Name, Amen.

He who covers his sins will not prosper, but whoever confesses and forsakes them will have mercy. **Proverbs 28:13**

Jesus said to him, "I am the way, the truth, and the life. No one comes to the Father except through Me. **John 14:6**

That if you confess with your mouth the Lord Jesus and believe in your heart that God has raised Him from the dead, you will be saved. 10 For with the heart one believes unto righteousness, and with the mouth confession is made unto salvation. **Romans 10:9-10**

Carol Clarke Ministries

A PRAYER ABOUT FORGIVENESS OF SINS

Dear Father, You said that if we confess all of our sins, You will be faithful and just to forgive us and to cleanse us from all unrighteousness. Holy One, I confess my sins this day and I ask that You will forgive me for the things in my life that do not mirror Your righteousness. Help me Lord to be thankful for your blood, which was shed for the remission of my sins. I therefore repent from my sinful habits and receive the gift of the Holy Spirit in Jesus Name.

If we confess our sins, He is faithful and just to forgive us our sins and to cleanse us from all unrighteousness. **1 John 1:9**

A PRAYER ABOUT HABITUAL SIN

Dear Father, sin makes us unrighteous in Your eyes and it is not Your will that we keep on sinning, because Your Word says that no one who abides in him keeps on sinning. Also if we keep on sinning, it means that we have not seen or known You. So Lord, I ask that You remove the desire of habitual sin in my life, because if I keep on practicing sin, then I am choosing to serve the enemy. But Father, I ask that you destroy the works of the devil over my life and let Your seed abide in me; this I pray, Amen.

Whoever abides in Him does not sin. Whoever sins has neither seen Him nor known Him. Little children, let no one deceive you. He who practices righteousness is righteous, just as He is righteous. He who sins is of the devil, for the devil has sinned from the beginning. For this purpose the Son of God was manifested, that He might destroy the works of the devil. Whoever has been born of God does not sin, for His seed remains in him; and he cannot sin, because he has been born of God. **1 John 3:6-10**

Carol Clarke Ministries

A PRAYER ABOUT SPIRITUAL AUTHORITY

El Shaddai (God Almighty), I bless You because You have given all believers power and authority that comes only from You. Help me Lord to exercise that authority that is within me, because greater is He that is in me, than he that is in the world. From this day forward, I shall walk in spiritual authority. I declare that through the Holy Spirit that works in me, I have power and authority over all demons in Jesus Name and nothing can hurt me, Amen.

He who is in you is greater than he who is in the world. **1 John 4:4**

And Jesus came and spoke to them, saying, "All authority has been given to Me in heaven and on earth. **Matthew 28:18**

Behold, I give you the authority to trample on serpents and scorpions, and over all the power of the enemy, and nothing shall by any means hurt you. **Luke 10:19**

A PRAYER ABOUT CHURCH MINISTRIES

Oh Lord my God, I thank You for every church and the ministries within them. Lord, in this prayer, I ask that every church ministry will function according to Your Will and purpose. Let every ministry leader take their responsibility seriously because it is the Holy Spirit that has made them overseers, to shepherd those which He purchased with His own blood. So God, I pray that you will awaken, men, women, children and youth ministries so that Your Name will be glorified, Amen.

Therefore, take heed to yourselves and to all the flock, among which the Holy Spirit has made you overseers, to shepherd the church [a]of God which He purchased with His own blood. **Acts 20:28**

Carol Clarke Ministries

A PRAYER ABOUT THE GIFT OF PROPHECY

Jehovah Elyon (The Most High), thank You for the gift of prophecy that is available to believers, according to Your Will. I come to You boldly requesting the prophetic gift to be released fully into my life. Lord, let Your divine Holy Spirit, teach me and guide me in the gift of prophecy because Your Word tells us that we should not despise prophecies. Help me not to abuse and misuse this gift, but to be humble in speaking what the Spirit brings to mind. Father, give divine revelation for the edifying of the Body of Christ and so that unbelievers will come to know You; this I pray, Amen.

Do not despise prophecies. **1 Thessalonians 5:20**

A PRAYER ABOUT THE ANOINTING OF GOD

Holy Father, thank You for Your Word, that reminds us that it is the Spirit of the Lord, that anoints us to preach the gospel to the poor, to release those who are in captivity and to set free those who are oppressed. Lord, let Your anointing be made manifest in every area of my life so that I can fulfil the mandate of heaven. Lord, I thank You because I know that I have the anointing of God that comes only from You, Amen.

"The Spirit of the Lord is upon Me, Because He has anointed Me To preach the gospel to the poor; He has sent Me to heal the brokenhearted, To proclaim liberty to the captives And recovery of sight to the blind, To set at liberty those who are oppressed. **Luke 4:18**

But you have an anointing from the Holy One, and you know all things. **1 John 2:20**

A PRAYER ABOUT REVELATION

To the only true and living God, if I call to You, You promised to answer me and to show me unsearchable things which I do not know. Father, I pray that I will be a place spiritually to receive Your divine revelation. Like John in Revelation 4, help me to remain in the spirit so that you can show me things which are yet to take place; Lord, I ask that You will reveal to me the things of heaven; this is the cry of my heart, Amen.

Immediately I was in the Spirit; and behold, a throne set in heaven, and One sat on the throne. **Revelation 4:2**

"Call to Me, and I will answer you, and show you great and mighty things, which you do not know." **Jeremiah 33:3**

A PRAYER FOR THE START OF A MEETING

Our Father who art in heaven, thank you for this meeting today. We ask that you strengthen, inspire and restore us during this meeting. Lord, give us strength and power, not a jumpstart but something long lasting like Duracell. Lord, Your Word reminds us that in the morning, you hear our voice. So during this meeting, we ask that as we lay our requests before you, you will hear us. Lord, we wait expectantly, depending on your strength and direction in this meeting. Our trust and confidence are completely in You and we ask that You inspire us to make godly decisions; this we ask, Amen.

My voice You shall hear in the morning, O Lord; In the morning I will direct it to You, and I will look up. **Psalm 5:3**

Carol Clarke Ministries

A PRAYER FOR THE END OF THE MEETING

Holy Father, as we come to the end of this meeting, we thank You for what you have done through us and for what has been accomplished. We thank You for the amazing things You have done today. May You bless the matters discussed and help us rise in You: moving upwards and never down so that we will be better people to serve those who we may meet. We bless You for the words you have sown into our hearts today. We are grateful that what has been sown will spring up and never die. Help us to recognise that You are always in control and that You are willing to lead us in all truth. Help us fan into flame the gift that you have given us. As we depart from one another, we thank You that you walk with us. For Thine is the Kingdom, the power and the Glory, forever and ever, Amen.

However, when He, the Spirit of truth, has come, He will guide you into all truth… **John 16:13**

Therefore, I remind you to stir up the gift of God which is in you through the laying on of my hands. **2 Timothy 1:6**

"… For Yours is the kingdom and the power and the glory forever, Amen." **Matthew 6:13**

A PRAYER ABOUT TEACHERS

Father we thank You for all our teachers, thanking You for their creativity, work ethic, commitment, drive and passion to those who they educate. Father, Your Word reminds us that those who are perfectly trained will be like their teacher. We ask that You bless those teachers who have contributed to the lives of others, inspiring them to become doctors, nurses, solicitors and educators. We appreciate, honour, respect and recognise teachers because they are the ones who see the best in the life of others and strives to make something beautiful out of it through education and creativity; thank You Lord, Amen.

A disciple is not above his teacher, but everyone who is perfectly trained will be like his teacher. **Luke 6:40**

Carol Clarke Ministries

A PRAYER ABOUT WOMEN IN BUSINESS

Dear Lord, I thank You for Your divine blessings over my business. I thank You for the creativity You have given me to become a successful businesswoman. I declare that I will remain steadfast in You and that I will seek first the Kingdom of God and Your righteousness because I know that all things shall be added to me. So, Lord I will not worry about tomorrow, because I know that You are in full control of this enterprise; So, thank You Lord, Amen.

But seek first the kingdom of God and His righteousness, and all these things shall be added to you. Therefore do not worry about tomorrow, for tomorrow will worry about its own things. Sufficient for the day is its own trouble. **Matthew 6:33-34**

A PRAYER ABOUT BUSINESS OPPORTUNITIES

Our Father, who art in heaven, hallowed be Your Name. Lord, I will remain faithful in this business and declare new openings and expansion, in Jesus Name. I pray for all those business entrepreneurs and the gifted skills You have placed within them to make all that the Lord has commanded. I pray that just as flowers grow and flourish, this business will also grow, creating new opportunities for those I come into contact with; thank You Lord, Amen.

All who are gifted artisans among you shall come and make all that the Lord has commanded. **Exodus 35:10**

A PRAYER ABOUT SUCCESS

Holy One, I speak Your Word into my life in that I can do all things through Christ who gives me strength. Father, I bless You because it is through You that I am prosperous and successful. Help me not to think that I have succeeded because of my own intellectual, but Lord I commit all that I do to You. May You establish my plans, so that all that I am, equates to success. May my primary goal be to always find success in the eyes of God. Let my life be pleasing to You God so that I can receive your blessings in abundance. Amen.

I can do all things through Christ who strengthens me. **Philippians 4:13**

Commit your works to the Lord, And your thoughts will be established. **Proverbs 16:3**

A PRAYER ABOUT A HUSBAND BLESSING HIS WIFE

Heavenly Father, I thank you for my wife today and the opportunity to break bread with her during this special meal. As we share in this meal, I also pray that Your blessings will follow her each day of her life and that she will never be in want. Father, may you meet all her needs according to the riches of Your glory. I also pray that You grant her the desires of her heart and that every plan that she has in life will come to past; thank You for My wife, Amen.

And my God shall supply all your need according to His riches in glory by Christ Jesus. **Philippians 4:19**

May He grant you according to your heart's desire, and fulfill all your purpose. **Psalm 20:4**

Carol Clarke Ministries

A PRAYER ABOUT A WIFE BLESSING HER HUSBAND

Oh Lord, I give You thanks today for my husband and I pray a special covering over him. May Your favour rest upon him and follow him all the days of his life. I pray that You will always establish the works of his hands and that everything he touches shall be blessed. I pray that no task will be too difficult for him and that he will trust You at all times. So, Lord as he continues to serve in the position of the head of the home, I pray that You will grant favour and divine strength that comes only from You, Amen.

And let the beauty of the Lord our God be upon us and establish the work of our hands for us; Yes, establish the work of our hands.
Psalm 90:17

A PRAYER ABOUT A FATHER'S BLESSING OVER HIS SON

Heavenly Father, I glorify Your Name as You have blessed me with a wonderful son. As his natural father, I pray that (name of son) grows into a young man that will be fruitful in all that he does and will walk in the power and dominion that You have given him. Father may he always know his identity in You and know that he is a child of the highest King. Bless him Lord, Amen.

Then God blessed them, and God said to them, "Be fruitful and multiply; fill the earth and subdue it; have dominion over the fish of the sea, over the birds of the air, and over every living thing that moves on the earth." **Genesis 1:28**

Carol Clarke Ministries

A PRAYER ABOUT A FATHER'S BLESSING OVER HIS DAUGHTER

Heavenly Father, thank You for my precious daughter. I pray today that You will pour out Your love upon her. May she be like a tree planted by the rivers of water that she will be prosperous in all that she does. Jesus, I ask that You anoint her hands for Your service and for Your glory. Let everything she sets her heart to, be accomplished because all things are possible through Christ who gives strength, Amen.

He shall be like a tree Planted by the rivers of water, that brings forth its fruit in its season, Whose leaf also shall not wither; and whatever he does shall prosper. **Psalm 1: 3**

I can do all things through Christ who strengthens me. **Philippians 4:13**

A PRAYER ABOUT A MOTHER'S BLESSING OVER HER SON

Heavenly Father, I bless Your Holy Name and I commit my dear son into Your loving hands. As the mother of (name of son), I pray that You will cover him from the crown of his head to the sole of his feet and that no weapon formed against him shall prosper. I pray that You will open the windows of heaven and bless him in ways that he could never imagine. I pray that everything he puts his hands to shall be blessed. So, Lord I ask for Your blessings upon (name of son) in Jesus Name, Amen.

No weapon formed against you shall prosper, and every tongue which rises against you in judgment You shall condemn. This is the heritage of the servants of the Lord, and their righteousness is from Me," Says the Lord. **Isaiah 54:17**

A PRAYER ABOUT A MOTHER'S BLESSING OVER HER DAUGHTER

Dear Father, I praise Your Name as You created my inmost being and You knitted my daughter together in my womb. Lord, I know that she is fearfully and wonderfully made. So, during this season, I pray that (name of daughter) will always be strong and courageous in all that she does and faces. Grant her with strength, wisdom and understanding that she will be effective at all times. As you bless her, I pray that You will always be with her guiding and directing her every footstep; thank You Father, Amen.

For You formed my inward parts; You covered me in my mother's womb. I will praise You, for I am fearfully and wonderfully made; Marvelous are Your works, and that my soul knows very well. **Psalm 139:13-14**

Have I not commanded you? Be strong and of good courage; do not be afraid, nor be dismayed, for the Lord your God is with you wherever you go." **Joshua 1:9**

Printed in Poland
by Amazon Fulfillment
Poland Sp. z o.o., Wrocław